Library Buddy

BY CAROL KIM
ILLUSTRATED BY FELIA HANAKATA

JOLLY
FiSH
PRESS
Mendota Heights, Minnesota

Book design by Jake Nordby
Illustrations by Felia Hanakata

Published in the United States by Jolly Fish Press, an imprint of North Star Editions, Inc.

First Edition
First Printing, 2019

Library of Congress Cataloging-in-Publication Data
Names: Kim, Carol, author. | Hanakata, Felia, illustrator.
Title: Library buddy / by Carol Kim ; illustrated by Felia Hanakata.
Description: First edition. | Mendota Heights, MN : Published in the United
   States by Jolly Fish Press, an imprint of North Star Editions, Inc., 2020.
   | Series: Doggie daycare | Summary: "Shawn and Kat Choi try to find a new
   activity that a goldendoodle with failing eyesight will love"— Provided
   by publisher.
Identifiers: LCCN 2019006811 (print) | LCCN 2019019201 (ebook) | ISBN
   9781631633379 (ebook) | ISBN 9781631633362 (pbk.) | ISBN 9781631633355
   (hardcover)
Subjects: | CYAC: Goldendoodle—Fiction. | Dogs—Fiction. | Animals with
   disabilities—Fiction. | Dog day care—Fiction. | Libraries—Fiction. |
   Moneymaking projects—Fiction. | Brothers and sisters—Fiction. | Korean
   Americans—Fiction.
Classification: LCC PZ7.1.K554 (ebook) | LCC PZ7.1.K554 Li 2019 (print) |
   DDC [Fic]—dc23
LC record available at https://lccn.loc.gov/2019006811

Jolly Fish Press
North Star Editions, Inc.
2297 Waters Drive
Mendota Heights, MN 55120
www.jollyfishpress.com

Printed in the United States of America

TABLE OF CONTENTS

CHAPTER 1

Buddy

"I can't believe you are going to tutor Joshua in reading!" Kat Choi said to her older brother, Shawn, while riding in the car.

"I couldn't say no to his parents," said Shawn.

"Joshua is behind in reading," their mother said. "He needs help."

"But he's so annoying!" Kat said.

"Once, I had to use the bathroom at recess. Now he calls me Princess Pee!"

"The best way to handle teasing is to ignore it," their father said.

"Or just call him Prince Potty," said Shawn.

Kat giggled.

The Choi family car stopped in front of a white house. Kat waved excitedly to her aunt and uncle and jumped out of the car.

"Where is Buddy?" Kat asked, looking for their goldendoodle.

"He's probably sleeping somewhere,"

their uncle said. "Buddy has been a little ... slower lately." He was choosing his words carefully. "Ever since he started losing his eyesight."

"You kids go inside and find him," their aunt suggested.

Shawn and Kat found Buddy sleeping in the back room.

"Hi, Buddy," Shawn said.

Buddy sat up, tail wagging.

"Let's play hide-and-seek," Kat said.

"I'm not sure he's up for that," Shawn said, looking at the dog's cloudy eyes.

"But it's his favorite game!" Kat said.

Shawn shrugged. "Okay, you hide first."

Kat climbed into the bathtub and hid behind the shower curtain. "Ready!" she called.

"Buddy, go find Kat!" Shawn said.

Buddy slowly walked out of the room, then sat.

"Buuudddeee!" called Kat.

Buddy yawned and lay down.

"Uh, Kat, I think Buddy is done with this game!" Shawn called.

Kat climbed out of the bathtub. "Poor Buddy," she said, hugging the dog.

The children led Buddy into the kitchen.

"Hey, kids," their aunt said. "Your mom says you have a doggie daycare business. Uncle David and I need someone to take care of Buddy for a month. Think you are up for it?"

"That would be awesome!" Shawn said.

"Wonderful!" their aunt said. "Let's do it!"

CHAPTER 2

Reading Enemies

Two weeks later, Shawn and Kat walked into the house with Buddy. Shawn sighed loudly as he hung up Buddy's leash.

"What's wrong?" their grandmother asked.

"Buddy doesn't want to walk or play or do *anything*," Shawn said.

"Poor thing," Halmoni said. She bent and gently patted Buddy's head.

"Remember, Joshua is coming today," she said to Shawn.

Kat groaned.

After Joshua arrived, Shawn led him to the kitchen table and handed him a book. "I thought we could start by reading together," he said.

Joshua read slowly, sounding out each word.

Kat walked in. She grabbed her stuffed owl and turned to leave.

"Gonna play with your dolls?" Joshua asked her.

"Stanley is an *owl*," Kat huffed.

"Stanley?" Joshua laughed. "That's a weird name for your owl doll."

Kat glared. Seeing one of her books on the table, she snapped, "This is my book!"

Snatching it up, she stomped down the hall.

Kat found Buddy lying down in the guest room closet.

"Hey, Buddy," Kat said. "Wanna go outside?"

Buddy's tail wagged a little, but he stayed in the closet.

Kat sighed. She sat on the floor nearby and opened the book she was holding.

"This is a Korean folktale," Kat said and began reading.

After a few minutes, Buddy poked his head out.

"You like the story?" Kat asked.

Buddy lay down next to Kat. She read some more.

She was still reading when Shawn appeared.

"What are you doing?" Shawn asked.

"Buddy likes listening to stories," Kat said. "It got him to leave the closet."

"Buddy the bookworm!" Shawn laughed.

CHAPTER 3

The Reading Challenge

"Let's go to the library and get some books about goldendoodles," Kat said later that week. "And about helping dogs who are going blind."

"Good idea," said Shawn. "We can bring Joshua."

"Ugh," said Kat.

"Hello, kids!" Mr. Perez, the librarian, said when the three children arrived.

"You are just in time to sign up for the summer reading challenge!"

"Great," muttered Joshua.

"Each week for a month, teams of three to four kids will read books I have selected," Mr. Perez said. "Every Saturday, there will be a trivia quiz. Prizes will go to the highest scoring teams."

"The three of us can be a team!" Shawn said.

Kat and Joshua groaned.

Shawn ignored them. "Sign us up!" Shawn said.

Later, the kids headed to the dog section.

"Goldendoodles are a mix of golden retrievers and poodles," Shawn read. "They are friendly and tend to cause fewer allergy symptoms."

"That definitely sounds like Buddy," said Joshua. "The friendly part, I mean."

Shawn nodded in agreement.

"Any ideas for how we can help Buddy?" asked Kat.

Shawn shook his head. "We have been doing everything the books suggest, like helping him learn the layout of the house and to use his other senses," he said.

"We need an activity that makes him happy," Kat said.

Shawn looked at Kat, thinking.

"Let's go back home now," he said. "There is something I want to try."

"Where is Buddy?" Kat asked Halmoni when they got home.

"I think he's sleeping in the closet, as usual," Halmoni said.

Shawn turned to Joshua. "I had an idea for helping Buddy. Can you read to him? It seems to cheer him up."

Joshua shrugged. "Okay. I guess."

Joshua went into the guest room, holding a book.

Several minutes later, Joshua came out. "Do you have another book?" he asked.

"Sure," Shawn said, handing him one.

"Joshua read both these books to Buddy," Shawn told Kat after Joshua left. "I think Joshua actually liked doing it."

Kat hugged the dog. "Good job, Buddy!"

CHAPTER 4

Teamwork

On Saturday, Shawn, Kat, Joshua, and Buddy walked to the library for story time. "Mr. Perez is having it in the courtyard so Buddy can come," Shawn said.

"Can I hold his leash?" Joshua asked.

"Sure," Kat said, handing it over.

"This must be Buddy," Mr. Perez said when they arrived.

"He really likes being read to," Shawn said.

"Can we add him to our team?" Kat asked.

"Absolutely!" Mr. Perez said.

"We can be Team Library Buddy!" Joshua said.

"That's a good idea!" Kat said to Joshua.

"Can I pet your dog?" asked a boy with blond hair.

"Sure," said Shawn.

Buddy wagged his tail.

Other kids came over. "Is he here for story time?" asked a girl with pigtails.

"Yep!" said Kat. "He loves stories!"

More children gathered around Buddy. His tail wagged faster and faster.

"Buddy loves this attention!" Kat said, smiling.

"Maybe there is a way for Buddy to be an official library visitor," said Shawn.

After story time was over, Mr. Perez stood up.

"For those doing the reading challenge, the trivia questions are inside at the front desk," he said.

After the quizzes were scored, Team Library Buddy was in second-to-last place.

"Next time, we will do better," Shawn said. "But we all have to read *all* of the books. Okay, Joshua?"

Joshua was silent for a moment. And then Buddy licked his hand, making Joshua laugh.

"Yeah, okay," Joshua said. "I promise I will read all the books next time."

The next day, the doorbell rang. Shawn and Kat were surprised to see it was Joshua.

Joshua gave an awkward wave. "I, uh, thought maybe Buddy would like to hear how the book I was reading to him ends," he mumbled.

Kat and Shawn stared at him.

Then Kat picked up the book and smiled. She handed it to Joshua. "Buddy would love that."

CHAPTER 5

Library Buddy

"Today is the final round," Shawn said two weeks later. "Let's do this!"

At the library, children ran to greet Buddy.

"Hi, Buddy!" "Yay! It's Buddy!" they cried.

Mr. Perez passed out the questions. "Please work alone," he said. "But you can work as a team on the bonus round."

Shawn read the bonus question to his teammates: "From the book *Wintertime at Wolf Lodge*, name two facts John and Allie learn about wolves."

"Uhhh," said Kat.

"Wolves live in packs," said Joshua.

"That's one," said Shawn.

"They can smell a hundred times better than humans," said Joshua.

"How did you remember those facts?" Kat asked Joshua.

"I read that book to Buddy three or four times," Joshua said. "It's his favorite."

After Mr. Perez tallied the results, everyone gathered to hear the winners announced.

"In third place . . . Team Rainbow Unicorns!" Mr. Perez said.

Four girls jumped up and cheered.

"Second place goes to . . . Team Library Buddy!"

"Whoo-hoo!" Shawn yelled.

Kat and Joshua grinned.

"And first place goes to . . . Team Fire and Ice!"

"YES!" Two boys fist-bumped while two girls hugged.

Later, Mr. Perez walked up to Shawn, Kat, and Joshua. "Your scores went up a lot at the end," he said. "You earned free ice cream for Most Improved!"

"Thanks!" Shawn said.

"Buddy was a big help," Kat said. "Joshua read to him a lot."

"Could Buddy be an official library visitor?" Shawn asked.

"I'm glad you asked," Mr. Perez said. "You could get him trained as a therapy dog."

"What's that?" Shawn asked.

"It is special training so he can visit places like schools, hospitals, or libraries," Mr. Perez said.

"Buddy would be great at that," Joshua said.

"Then Buddy could come to the library more often!" cried Kat.

"That's what I was hoping," Mr. Perez said. "I have been wanting to start a reading program with dogs. Maybe Buddy could be our first volunteer."

"He does make a great reading buddy," Joshua said.

"You could call it *Library Buddies!*" Kat giggled. "How do you like that, Buddy?"

Buddy wagged his tail.

Then she turned to Joshua and held up her ice cream coupon. "Want to get some ice cream with us tomorrow?"

Joshua's eyes widened.

"Any friend of Buddy's is a friend of mine," Kat said, grinning.

"Sure," said Joshua. "Team Library Buddy *rocks!*"

THINK ABOUT IT

🐾 Joshua likes to tease Kat. Tell about a time you were teased and how it made you feel.

🐾 Shawn, Kat, and Joshua take part in a reading challenge. Plan a reading challenge of your own. See if you can get a friend to join in on the fun!

🐾 Buddy will be trained as a therapy dog. Research service dogs at your local library. What are five jobs that dogs can do?

ABOUT THE AUTHOR

Carol Kim lives in Texas with her husband, two daughters, and one very well-behaved dog. Her childhood was spent in Southern California, where she grew up eating kimchi every day. She writes both fiction and nonfiction for children. When she's not writing, she enjoys reading, cooking, traveling, and exploring food from different cultures.

ABOUT THE ILLUSTRATOR

Felia Hanakata is an Indonesia-based illustrator. She went to the Academy of Art University and completed her BFA in illustration in spring 2017. She thinks storytelling breathes life and colors into the world. When she is not drawing, she usually reads, drinks lots of coffee, plays video games, or looks for inspiration in nature and her surroundings.

Strangling Your
Husband Is **NOT**
an Option